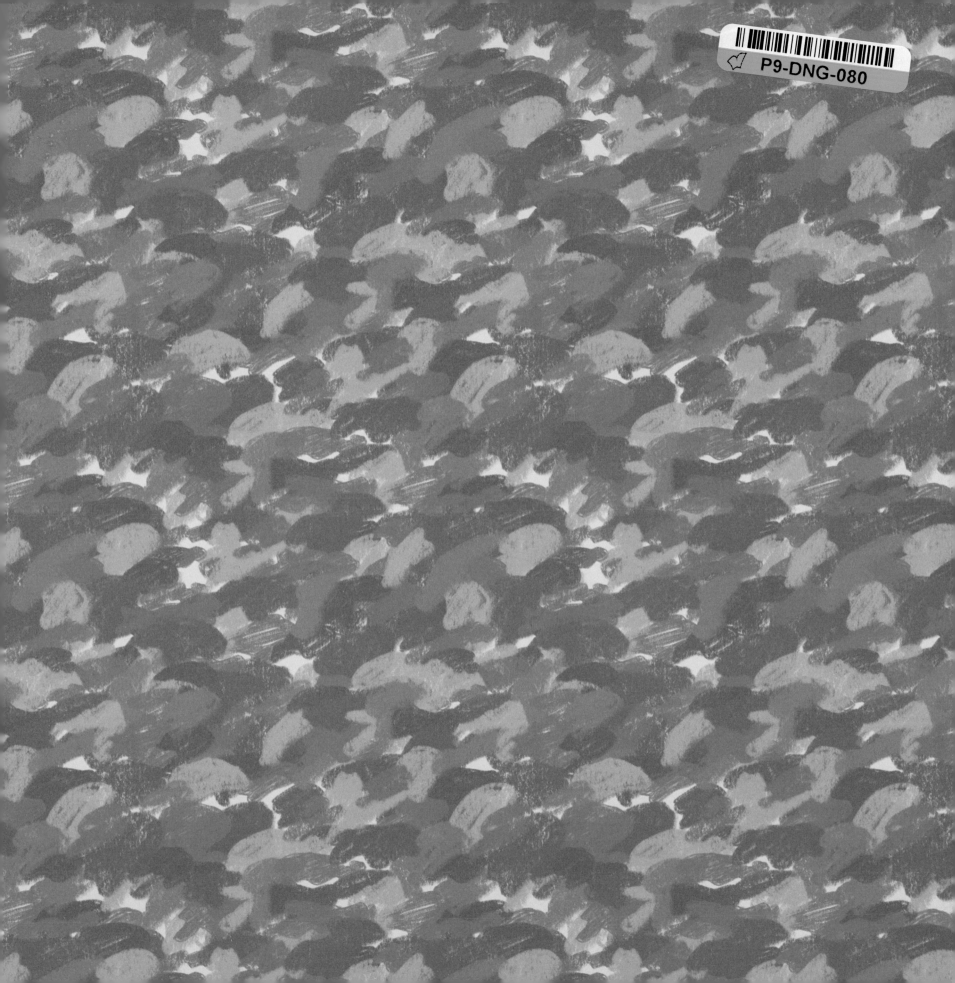

For Dad

H.T.

With thanks to Renee, for her invaluable
suggestions, and for her service.

First American Edition 2018
Kane Miller, A Division of EDC Publishing
PO Box 470663, Tulsa, OK 74147-0663
www.kanemiller.com
Text by Isabel Otter
Text copyright © Caterpillar Books 2018
Illustrations copyright © Hannah Tolson 2018
Library of Congress Control Number: 2017948139
978-1-61067-720-2
Printed in China
CPB/1400/1065/1118
10 9 8 7 6 5 4 3 2

My Daddy is a
Hero

Illustrated by *hannah tolson*

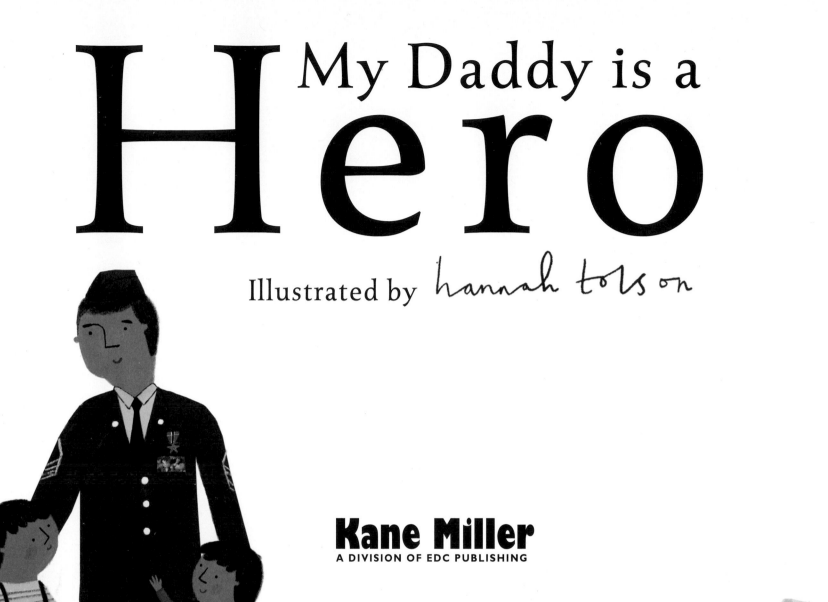

Kane Miller
A DIVISION OF EDC PUBLISHING

My daddy is a hero, he stands out from the crowd.

He's there to keep
our country safe

and makes us very proud.

My daddy is a hero,

a master of the skies.

A skillful navigator,

calm every time he flies.

My daddy is a hero,

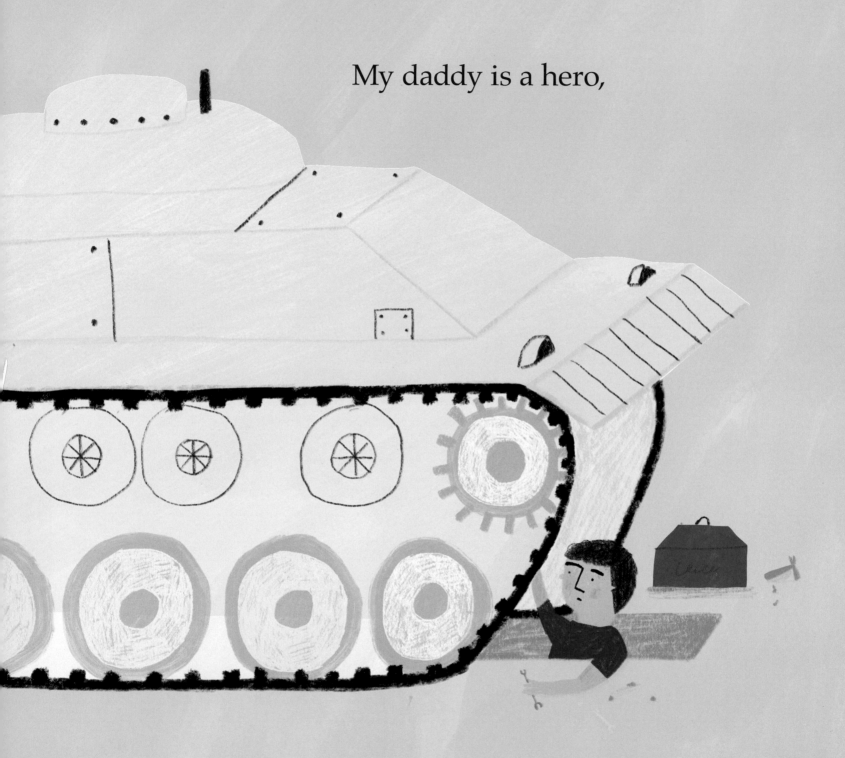

he fixes broken things.

Any sort of vehicle,

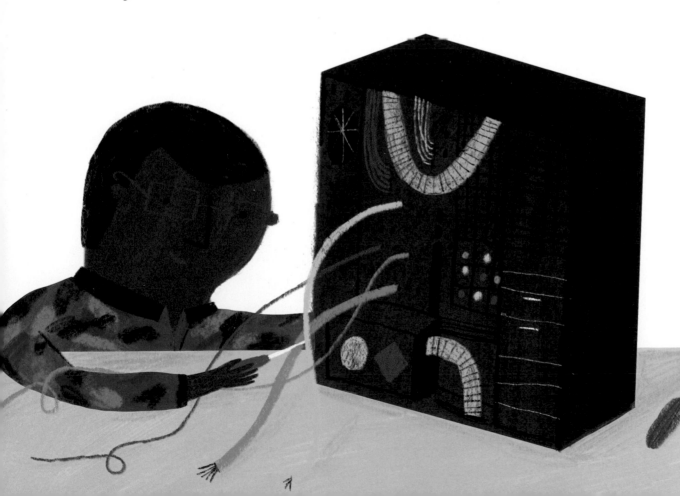

whatever each
day brings.

My daddy is a hero, he sails the seven seas.

And anytime I need him,

he's always there for me.

My daddy is a hero,
he cares for those in need.

Anyone who seeks his trust

will find a friend indeed.

My daddy is a hero,

he's full of bravery.

I'll follow in his footsteps and make him proud of me.

My daddy is a hero, there's nowhere he won't go.

He helps out those
who need him

in rain, hot sun
or snow.

My daddy is a hero,

he helps the
sick all day.

And when I'm
feeling poorly,

he takes my pain away.

My daddy is a hero,
watching traffic way up high.

He keeps a lookout all around
as Air Force planes fly by.

My daddy is a hero,
he brings music to our ears.

When I hear him play his flute,
it melts away my fears.

My daddy is a hero,

he inspires me
every day.

His heart goes
into all he does –

at work and
then at play.

My daddy is a hero,

he stands out
from the crowd.

He's there to keep our country safe
and makes us very proud.